21st Century Junior Library

Trees WITHDRAWN

By Jennifer Colby

CHERRY LAKE PUBLISHING * ANN ARBOR, MICHIGAN

Published in the United States of America by Cherry Lake Publishing
Ann Arbor, Michigan
www.cherrylakepublishing.com

Consultants: Elizabeth A. Glynn, Youth Education Coordinator, Matthaei Botanical
Gardens and Nichols Arboretum, University of Michigan; Marla Conn, ReadAbility, Inc.

Photo Credits: © javarman /Shutterstock Images, cover, 6; © LehaKoK /Shutterstock Images, 4;
© apinunrin /Shutterstock Images, 8; © Alexey Stiop /Shutterstock Images, 10; © TaMaNKunG /
Shutterstock Images, 12; © FotograFFF /Shutterstock Images, 14; © kak2s /Shutterstock Images, 16;
© paulz /Shutterstock Images, 18; © Nina B/Shutterstock Images, 20

LIBRARY OF CONGRESS CATALOGING-IN-PUBLICATION DATA
Colby, Jennifer, 1971-
  Trees/by Jennifer Colby. – [Revised edition]
     pages cm.—(21st century junior library)
  Includes bibliographical references and index.
  ISBN 978-1-63188-041-4 (hardcover)—ISBN 978-1-63188-127-5 (pdf)—
ISBN 978-1-63188-084-1 (pbk.)—ISBN 978-1-63188-170-1 (ebook)
  1. Trees–Juvenile literature. I. Title. II. Series: 21st century junior library.
SD391.C66 2014
635.9'77–dc23   2014006228

Cherry Lake Publishing would like to acknowledge the work of
The Partnership for 21st Century Skills.
Please visit www.p21.org *for more information.*

Printed in the United States of America

CONTENTS

Some giant redwood trees are more than 100 feet (30 meters) wide!

Amazing Trees

Did you know that trees are some of the biggest living things on Earth? Giant redwood trees are as tall as a 30-story building. They can be more than 300 feet (91 meters) tall. They can live for up to 2,000 years!

The trees in your neighborhood may not be as tall as **skyscrapers**. They may not be **ancient**. But all trees are special. Let's take a closer look at trees.

The leaves of many broad-leaved trees
turn bright colors in the fall.

Grouping Trees

There are many kinds of trees. **Scientists** put them into two groups: broad-leaved trees and **conifers**. The leaves of trees can help you decide which group a tree is in. Broad-leaved trees have wide, flat leaves. Maple and oak trees are in this group. They lose their leaves in the fall. New leaves grow in the spring. They are **deciduous** trees.

Conifers have thin and pointy leaves
called needles.

Conifer trees can have thin, pointy leaves. These leaves are called needles. Spruce and pine trees have needles. They are conifers. Cedar and juniper trees are also conifers. But their leaves are flat and scaly. Many conifers keep their leaves through the winter. They are **evergreen** trees.

The fruit of a peach tree is soft and juicy.
The seed is inside the peach.

Both groups of trees make seeds. A seed can grow a new plant. Conifers have seeds inside their cones. Broad-leaved trees have seeds inside their fruit. Some fruits are juicy and soft. Some fruits have seeds inside a hard shell.

Look!

Go for a walk. Ask an adult to join you. Look at the different trees around you. Can you tell which are broad-leaved trees and which are conifers? Remember to look at their leaves to give you clues.

The roots of some trees are very large.
They grow deep into the ground.

Trees Are Strong!

Tree roots can grow deep into the dirt. They hold the tree in the ground. Roots also absorb water. The water moves up the trunk of the tree. It goes through the branches of the tree to all of the leaves.

The trunk is a hard stem. It is made of wood. **Bark** is the hard covering on the trunk and the branches. The bark protects the tree.

The wood we use to build a house
comes from trees.

Branches and leaves shape the **crown** of the tree. The crown makes shade on the ground below.

A tree's trunk and branches grow as the tree gets older. The wood of trees is strong. We use the wood of trees to build many things.

Ask Questions!

Do you use paper at home and at school? Paper is made from trees. Find out how you can **recycle** paper at home and at school. If you recycle paper, you will save trees.

The leaves on this tree use sunlight to make food.

Inside Leaves

A large maple tree can grow more than 20,000 leaves each year. Why does it grow so many leaves?

Trees need energy to grow. But trees can't eat food to get energy like people do. Trees make their own food. The leaves of trees use the energy from sunlight to make food from air and water. Food is made inside the leaves. This is called **photosynthesis**.

The leaf of a maple tree has many veins.

Look at a deciduous leaf. It has many **veins**. The veins carry water into the leaf. The veins also carry food out of the leaf. The food goes out to all parts of the tree. The tree uses the energy from the food to grow and make seeds. A tree needs many leaves to make all the food it needs.

Different types of trees grow in different parts of the world.

Trees are all around us. There are many different kinds of trees. All trees use energy from sunlight to live and grow.

Create!

Collect leaves from your neighborhood. Then lay them on a table. Put a sheet of white paper on top of them. Carefully rub the side of a crayon over the paper. An outline of your leaves will show on the paper!

GLOSSARY

ancient (AYN-chuhnt) very old

bark (BARK) the outside layer on the trunk of a tree

conifers (KOH-nuh-ferz) trees that grow seeds in cones

crown (KROUN) the top of a tree shaped by its branches and leaves

deciduous (dih-SIJ-oo-uhs) a plant that loses its leaves every year

evergreen (EV-er-green) a plant that keeps its leaves through the year

photosynthesis (foh-toh-SIN-thi-sis) the process of using light energy to combine air and water to make a plant's food

recycle (ree-SY-kuhl) to use something old in order to make something new

scientists (SYE-uhn-tists) people who study the world around us by observing, experimenting, and measuring

skyscrapers (SKYE-skray-purz) very tall buildings

veins (VAYNZ) tubes that carry water into a leaf and food out of a leaf

FIND OUT MORE

BOOKS

Ingoglia, Gina. *The Tree Book: For Kids and Their Grown-Ups*. Brooklyn, NY: Brooklyn Botanic Garden, 2008.

Mellett, Peter. *Find Out About Trees*. North Wales, PA: Armadillo Books, 2013.

WEB SITES

Arbor Day Foundation— Life of a Tree
www.arborday.org/kids/carly/lifeofatree/
Learn about the rings of a tree and how they grow.

Arbor Day Foundation— Tree Identification
www.arborday.org/trees/whattree/WhatTree.cfm?ItemID=E6A
A step-by-step guide to help you identify a North American tree.

INDEX

ABOUT THE AUTHOR

Jennifer Colby is a school librarian, and she also has a bachelor's degree in Landscape Architecture. By writing these books, she has combined her talents for two of her favorite things. She likes to garden and grow her own food. In June she makes strawberry jam for her children to enjoy all year long.